# Her shoes are brown
### and other stories

# Her shoes are brown
## and other stories

Listeners: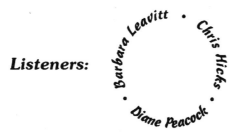

A Project of the Community Involvement Council

Canadian Cataloguing in Publication data
Hicks, Chris, 1958-
    Her shoes are brown and other stories
Includes bibliographical references.
ISBN 0 - 9694379 - 3 - 5
1. Handicapped - Rehabilitation - Ontario.
I. Leavitt, Barbara, 1962-  . II. Peacock, Diane, 1958-  .
III. Community Involvement Council (Milverton, Ont.). IV. Title.
HV1559.C2H53 1993     305.9'0816     C93-093915-8


Funding for this book, was provided in part by a grant from:

 Ministry of
Community and
Social Services
Ontario


Designed, typeset and bound by Thames Label & Litho, St. Marys.

For information on ordering this book, please write:
    STORIES
    Community Involvement Council
    Box 344
    Tillsonburg, Ontario, Canada
    N4G 4H8

 Printed on recycled paper

# *Who we are*

*T*he Community Involvement Council is an active group made up of staff representing human service agencies from several counties in southwestern Ontario. Our monthly meetings provide a forum for sharing ideas and resources. By recognizing the importance of listening to people's stories, we have grown both professionally and personally.

Our journey to provide a platform for the sharing of stories began three years ago. Now, we proudly offer this compilation highlighting people's struggles and successes to be full participants in our communities.

It's funny, when it comes to saying thank you, people don't want their names in print. Too bad. You were there for us with your warm hearts, cold eyes and red pens. What a team! Thanks Bud Carter, Bill Gow, Tricia Morris, Sara Thorne, Helen Watson, Marty Graf and especially Frank Moore for believing in us.

We are also grateful for the contributions of the "way back when" editorial committee of the Community Involvement Council who helped this book grow. Thanks to Cheri Emerson for her enthusiasm and hard work in the early stages.

To Win Schell and Linda Gregson, our editors, we thank you for going beyond the editing, and sharing your expertise.

Our appreciation goes out to our employers who have supported our efforts in the writing of this book: Forward House of London; Tillsonburg and District Association for Community Living; Stratford Area Association for Community Living.

And to all the members of the Community Involvement Council who waited and waited and waited...it's finally here!

**Thanks!**

    Chris Hicks       Barbara Leavitt       Diane Peacock

*Dedicated to people*
*who have courage*
*to share their stories*
*and to people*
*who have courage*
*to listen...*

# Her shoes are brown
## and other stories

# *notes to the reader*

*T*here are different ways of hearing a story. In collecting and writing stories for this book, we heard personal accounts told through gestures, through words, through family or friends, and through smiles. We have been privileged to experience many ways of listening. People invited us into their living rooms and their lives. They shared challenges and triumphs with us in their own ways.

We all face challenges. It may be fighting a system, discrimination, or personal barriers. Each challenge is different. This book celebrates journeys that include all of us. Journeys that we can recognize as both our own, and as those of people around us. These stories have touched our hearts with their beauty, and our minds with what they can teach us.

In the past few years, more and more people are telling their stories. And more and more people are listening. This book is also about listening, opening our eyes and our selves so that we find our humanness. It is about having the courage to listen and recognize that as community members, we share the journey.

One of our greatest fears is that people will read this book and find excuses. "These are exceptional people. It would never work for me. Or people I know. Or people I support. Or my son or daughter." This would be tragic. These stories are about people who believe in themselves, and people who believe in others. They are our neighbours, co-workers and friends. They are ourselves. These stories are from people in towns and cities across Ontario.

We have experienced a metamorphosis in ourselves and others throughout this process of listening to people. We, and those around us are more willing to share, we can sense it in our communities. It's very much like a barnraising. People need each other to get that barn built. People come together for a common goal. Neighbours need to rely on neighbours. Everyone has a part to play. It's time to celebrate the barns we are raising in our own neighbourhoods.

Each story in this collection is a snapshot of right now. It will be a different story next week or next year. Life is never perfect and we never really finish the journey.

People trusted us to reflect the truth of their stories. And their faith was inspiring. When one person was asked if she would like to hear the notes of her story after an interview, she said, "No thanks, I'll wait for the movie."

Thanks to all of you.

*Chris, Barbara, Diane*

# we all have a story

We forget the importance of celebrating people's stories. No matter how big or small, everything is a celebration.

People haven't been allowed to tell their stories. They haven't been listened to for so long. It means that there is no history. I hope many people will listen to these stories.

I have a story too. I'd like to tell it because I want people to know it's okay to share their story. I say to them, "Don't feel bad. It's part of your history and your own identity. It is important to tell your story."

For the first 20 years of my life, I lived at home. My mom was told to put me in an institution but my father, brother and sister said, "No way." I went to regular school, and got into regular trouble! I told my teachers what to do if I had a seizure. I can't thank my father enough for not letting them put me in a segregated school or class.

I was having a lot of convulsions. A whole bunch of us, my family and friends and the minister and his family, talked about what to do about it. Somebody said an institution would be a last resort. When we looked around, nobody offered services for people over 18 years of age.

Well, I did go into the institution. For the first few weeks, I was told I could leave when I wanted. My first doctor died. Then, the second doctor died and the good times changed into horrible times. I became a number on a piece of paper. I wasn't given a choice anymore. They never did get the seizures under control.

On my 21st birthday, I was looking forward to voting for the first time. I wanted to know the politicians and their views on issues. I was told that I couldn't vote. I was told that I had no rights now that I lived in the institution.

I was 18 years there. I figure I spent nine of those years locked up because I was a "rebel rouser". They thought they'd try and break my spirit. Their psychology didn't work. The more they fought against me, the more I fought against them.

One day, when I was lined up for lunch, a staff said, "Peter, go back to your room after lunch and pack because you're leaving at 1:30." I was moving. My parents hadn't even been told.

I moved to a group home in a small town for almost a year. Then I started telling people what *I* wanted. I told them plump and plain that I wanted an apartment. I came in with a list of everything I wanted. Surprise, surprise! I pretty well got what I asked for.

And here I am today. One of the most important things to remember is even though a story might sound horrendous, people actually lived it and are still alive today.

I hope agencies that provide services to people with disabilities will get the message. There are other things besides pushing paper that are important, such as listening to the people they support.

I hope families get the message that they need to be involved in helping their family member make decisions. Nobody makes decisions in isolation.

I hope educators get the message that people can learn, given proper supports. All kids should be together. Kids learn from each other.

Everyone has a story to tell. Listening is the key. Hearing just goes in one ear and out the other. Listening is stopping in the middle and taking action. If you don't take action, what's the point?

Peter Park
Project Coordinator
People First of Canada

# growing in circles

One of the basics in life is having people to count on. Not being alone. Circles of family and friends are about including people in our lives who we can turn to and trust. A circle can include relatives, neighbours, friends. The beauty is not what the relationship is, but that people care about each other.

Some circles are developed in a formal way with help from a support worker. Others are casual and tend to grow more naturally. It doesn't matter *how* it is started, as long as it is started. It will happen when people come together. It will happen by listening, respecting, and allowing everyone to give and take in different ways.

Instead of going in circles, without the involvement of family and friends, people in the following stories tell us of growing in circles.

*Sometimes, it's hard to believe in people. For Gail, Harry and their children Adam and Melinda, it was a challenge to believe in Irene. She had spent all her life in an institution and had a history of aggression. But this family welcomed Irene as a new member.*

*In meeting with them, I worked hard at trying to get to the magic that makes this family work. They insist they're nothing special. Yet each has recollections of getting used to life with Irene.*

*When Irene first moved in, Melinda was eight years old. She remembers being physically attacked. Now she says, "I consider Irene part of the family. It's no big deal." In listening to Adam talk about a recent argument he had with Irene, it strikes me that the beauty of this family is that it is like any other. There is arguing as well as respect, opposition as well as love. And in the daily challenges that family life inevitably brings, there is also acceptance. This comes out so clearly as Gail tells their story.*

*I* remember the first two weeks Irene spent with us. She was very aggressive towards both Harry and me, as well as the kids. When she got angry, she would break windows. One day she took off from the house and headed down the street. When Harry went after her and she lay down and started kicking him, it took the two of us to lift her up and pretty well drag her back to the house. A man walked by and Irene started screaming, "Help mister, they're trying to kill me! Call the police." We can laugh about it now, but I waited three days expecting the police to come!

Harry and I had both worked in institutions. We understood how difficult life was for people living there, and we wanted to help at least one person come out. So eight years ago, we contacted the Family Home Program at a local institution about having someone live with us. They were pretty excited about our interest and within a couple of weeks had someone in mind. We had no idea what Irene was like. All we were told was her age, that she had been born in the institution and that she had no family. We were also told that she had acted out before, but it had been years before.

The day we met Irene was the day she moved in. A big station wagon pulled up and out came Irene and the social workers. We went inside the house, sat around the kitchen table and talked. I remember Irene drinking a gallon of coffee and being pretty quiet. She just sat there, picking at her skin.

The first two months were hell. Irene had no sense of modesty. She would run around naked and take six baths a day. She would lash out physically at us and at the kids. She would scream and break windows. The final straw for me was when she attacked Melinda while she was holding a friend's baby. I thought, "My God, if Irene lashed out at the kids while they were on the staircase, they could be killed." I told Harry that she wasn't staying because I was scared for all of us. Harry was adamant that we needed to give Irene more time. He kept saying that if you give anyone enough time, they could change. She had lived in an institution for 43 years and couldn't be expected to adjust overnight. I agreed, reluctantly.

It did take time. After all, Irene had no concept of family life. When she got upset, she would yell, "I'm going to tell the doctor about you and he'll put you in a strait jacket and give you a hypo." Sometimes she would even say, "I can't help it. I had too much medication as a child and my brain doesn't work anymore."

Irene did not understand "family". She used to ask, "Who's on tonight?" as if Harry and I were staff. After living with us for over a year, Irene asked me if I had any kids. I explained that Melinda and Adam were our kids and that's why they lived here. Her response was, "Why do you keep me Gail? Do you like me?" I wanted to show that I did care, but I couldn't hug her. She refused to be touched. She would pull back almost as if she were afraid she was going to be hit.

The turning point came one day when Harry was sitting at the kitchen table. Irene pointed down and said teasingly that there was money on the floor. When Harry immediately looked, Irene laughed and said, "Fooled you!" We knew then she was beginning to feel comfortable. She's got a great sense of humour now. But for the first five years, Irene was very insecure. So many times she asked if we were going to send her back.

One day last summer, Irene said, "I can stay with you forever if I want, can't I Gail?" I looked at her. She was grinning ear to ear. It doesn't sound like much, but if you'd been there... She looked so happy, so radiant.

A couple of years ago, a social worker happened to see Irene at lunch time on a visit to the local Association for Community Living. I heard the astonishment in her voice when she said, "My God, is that Irene? Who's got her? It used to take five staff to hold her down." She couldn't believe Irene was "still out" in the community.

A few years after Irene moved in with us, we learned that her sister wanted to get in touch with her. It seemed that Irene's mother, as well as her two sisters and a brother, had been trying to find Irene. Her brother and sisters hadn't known that Irene even existed. After many phone calls and arrangements, Irene met her family. She sees them a few times a year now. At one point, her sister wanted Irene to live closer to her. But after spending a few days with us, she phoned and said she felt Irene was already living with family and wanted her to stay with us.

Irene enjoys having her own room and helping with chores. She's always telling us that she'll "mind the things" in the house while we're out. And she likes to be hugged now! She loves being part of the family.

I honestly can't remember the last time Irene became aggressive, but it was more than three years ago. She's so different now. She's involved in the community and has hobbies. Adam and Melinda's friends often ask if Irene can join them when they go out. Adam's girlfriend likes Irene and spends time with her doing crafts. Irene reminds you of a sweet little lady. It's hard to believe that she was so angry before. We don't take credit for any of this. I feel that all we did was provide the opportunities. Irene did all the rest.

I'll never forget when we were doing dishes together and Irene called me "Mom". She smiled and watched for my reaction like a shy child. I smiled back. I think it was her way of saying, "I belong."

*As Jeff's friend, I care about his future. I couldn't
imagine Jeff in "services". Two years ago, I talked to
Jeff and his mother and father about the idea of
forming a circle of friends. I phoned all over the place
trying to find out how to go about it. What I discovered
was that there is no special formula. Jeff's parents saw
that too. But as Jean says in her story, she and Bob, her
husband, were willing to see what could happen when
people simply come together.*

*I* guess it's easy for the years to slip by. Bob and I always thought Jeff would leave
the family home when he was in his twenties, like our other boys. But every birthday
came and went and, because we are not comfortable with handing Jeffrey completely
over to our local services, he continues to live at home. For 20 years, I have been
actively involved with the local Association for Community Living but I haven't seen
any residential services I would choose for Jeff because he has autism and needs 24
hour support. The main thing is our fear of losing control. What will he eat? Who will
shampoo his hair? What if he doesn't like the people he will live with? Will he regress?
If you ask people, you get the standard answers: "He'll be looked after. Yes, you can
come visit, just check with us first." And that awful patronizing, "Now, don't you
worry."

I do realize that I'm overprotective of Jeff and I do too much for him. I also know
that when he's in a different setting he can become more independent. Everyone talks
so much about choice now. We're concerned that staff might say Jeff has a choice
about, for example, having his teeth brushed. As much as he hates it, he doesn't have
a choice! Jeff doesn't understand why he needs to brush his teeth. It's not fair to call
that choice.

We realize and accept that when Jeff has his own place and support staff, he won't
get the same personal care as he does at home. But staff have power over people. It
worries us because so few people who need 24 hour support can express their wants,
needs, pain, or preferences. We know the staff are good people, and it's not that they

wouldn't do a good job, but it is just a job to them. It concerns us that staff might get angry with Jeff over something he may have no control over because they don't know enough about autism to understand him fully.

We would gladly keep Jeff at home, but we know it wouldn't be fair for him or his brothers to have to make a major adjustment when we die and he is 50 years old. Mike, Shawn and Kevin, Jeff's brothers, have always been very supportive, and have always been there when we needed them. We don't want them to have to take the full responsibility. They have their own lives too. We're in a routine now at home, but it wouldn't be fair to Jeff to have to deal with a traumatic move on top of a crisis.

We'd feel better if there were choices, like choosing a University. We aren't comfortable with putting Jeff on a waiting list, but what other choice do we have?

That's what we were thinking when a friend of Jeff's started talking to us about a circle of friends. She told us about other people and places where it was working. She showed us we didn't have to follow the crowd and go the conventional route - that there are other options most parents aren't aware of. We didn't know a whole lot about circles, but we went ahead. Bob and Jeff and I met with her and started a list of people who might be interested in developing a friendship with Jeff. It included everyone from old teachers and neighbours to former staff who used to work with Jeff. She did all the calling because I was uncomfortable with phoning and asking people if they were interested in being involved in Jeff's life. I think parents from my era don't like to ask for help. Maybe younger parents don't feel that way.

The circle started out as a way for Jeff to have more contact with different people and situations. Jeff's life has become more enriched through his circle. His world now reaches beyond the boundaries of home and the day services of the Association.

Jeff's friends have made a difference to his life. He's made real progress. He never used to stay up until midnight like he did the other night when he played pool, and went dancing with his friends. I think other people see Jeff more as a person with real needs and interests, because he's seen with his friends at different places around town. Jeff has become much more sociable. If someone comes to the house, he'll come out of his room and sit with us now. He would never have done that before. He'll even offer company a cup of tea!

He has things to look forward to now. We have a calendar where I mark Jeff's dates. He always brings me the pen and wants me to write names down. He knows it means he's going out with a friend.

When he stays overnight with friends, it's hard to describe the feeling of not having to be home right at 4:00 p.m. I don't feel I have to be on a strict schedule. It's like a weight is off my shoulders. I don't have to always be wondering what he's doing. It's such a constant thing. When Jeff's friends make plans with him, it gives me the freedom that most parents of adult children take for granted.

Bob and I decided to turn to Jeff's friends for help in planning for Jeff's future. The circle began to meet monthly and talk about Jeff's dreams and future living arrangements. There are usually 13 or 14 family and friends at our meetings. We also invited a representative from the local Association to sit in so we could establish a relationship with the agency. My biggest fear was that the circle wouldn't last, or that it was an "in" thing for the 90's. I'm still afraid that people could move and not be replaced, and then we would be back to where we started. But Jeff's friends have made a strong commitment.

We've looked into different options and have submitted a proposal for individualized funding for Jeff. We've been told there's no money right now, but we've been encouraged to continue. We know we will have to work with a local agency to administer support services. The difference is that we, Jeff's family along with his friends, will play the most important role. Jeff with his family and friends will be the planners in his life, and paid people will implement those plans. We definitely want to be part of the hiring of staff. We see Jeff's staff as part of the circle, part of the team.

If there were no circle, we would probably be the same as we were three years ago, saying, "Well, maybe next year..." If the Association had phoned and said there was an opening for Jeff, I don't know what we would have done. I know we can never say, "This is it." The circle can never be too big and his friends and family should always be welcoming new people. The most important thing is that we now feel that Jeff's family and friends will make sure he is happy. They know him and will be able to see and feel it.

I believe we can all work together for Jeff. As Bob said at one of Jeff's circle get togethers, "The Association brings the brains, we (the family) bring the heart, and you guys (friends) bring the soul!"

*Brenda's hope of regaining what she once had appeared to be a faded dream. How can you dream if you have to rely on paid staff to do everything for you? How can you envision a different life if people tell you that you need 24 hour care? How do you start believing in yourself?*

*Brenda will tell you.*

*F*or three months, I experienced a prickly sensation in my left hand. Neither my doctor nor I knew what was causing this numbness, but I sensed that something was definitely wrong.

It was a cold November morning. The kids had got on the school bus and I got ready to go to the hospital for some tests. I was thinking about what I would make for supper that night. As my mother-in-law drove me to the hospital, we talked about when we would start our Christmas shopping.

After the series of tests that day, the doctor decided I'd better stay. I was not going home. Within a few days, I learned I had a brain tumour.

Christmas is supposed to be a happy time for people. However, that Christmas turned out to be a Christmas filled with uncertainty and grief. On that Christmas Eve, a host of doctors operated on my brain. The surgery revealed the tumour was benign, but while I was on the operating table, I suffered a stroke. The stroke left me paralysed on one side of my body.

In the seven years spent hospitalized, I stood on the sidelines while my three sons grew up. My physical disabilities made it impossible to do many of the things most parents take for granted. No longer could I tuck my children into bed at night. Instead, nurses were needed to tuck me in. No longer could I pick up and hold my young ones, or race with them, or build Lego Blocks, or do the thousands of things I wanted to do.

My impaired speech made it difficult to communicate with my children. Even the most simple words were a struggle to get out. Making others understand those words, was, and still is, a chore. Most of my former friends unintentionally disappeared from my life, one by one. My marriage ended in divorce. The stroke claimed many of the pieces that made me the woman I was.

But mine is a success story. I have found, within myself, qualities of strength and persistence. I am an example of what can be achieved through sheer determination and with the help of people who care.

While living in the hospital, it felt like I was removed from the outside world. My life was dictated by nurses' schedules, when to bathe, when to eat, when I could go to the bathroom. There were times that I thought, "Well, this is what life will be for me." Until, one day, Diane came into my room. She explained to me that she was working on a project within her association that would assist people to develop their personal networks. I did not have a clue what the hell that meant!

The first few weeks, Diane and I spent time getting to know one another. It was hard finding places in the hospital to do that. We would go out of the hospital and that helped because my senses came alive. I started to have a different feeling about things. The days and weeks that followed were full of excitement and scepticism. With the help of Grace, the discharge co-ordinator of the hospital, and Diane, my personal support network started to take shape. Members of my support circle were people I had gotten to know at the hospital and through my church.

After a few meetings, Byron, who was part of my circle, asked me an interesting question. If I had the choice of living anywhere in the world, where would it be? I found it interesting because as far as I knew at the time, my only option was to move away to another community into a facility. In fact, I was already on their three-year waiting list.

Guess what I chose? That's right. I wanted to stay in my own community. Fancy that!

Very quickly the wheels began turning. Sue helped me make an application to Ontario Housing. Pastor Gene talked with people in our church. Soon many of my church acquaintances began pulling together things that I needed for an apartment. The only thing I owned was an old dresser that I could lock my personal things in.

Jackie was my emotional strength. When she finished her shift, she would come up to my ward and we would talk about very personal things.

Grace worked at getting Home Care supports. Fiona took me to an Ontario Housing Apartment Complex. Fiona was a physiotherapist I was introduced to four months before moving. She volunteered to help me figure out whether or not I could physically live on my own. Fiona had no doubt that I could do it, but I can't say I felt so confident at that time. Fiona, to this day, comes over once in a while for a cup of tea.

Jane, a member of the Lioness Club, convinced other members to financially support my transition. In fact, Jane called the Lions Club and they helped me purchase my first wheelchair. As luck would have it, six weeks before I moved, Jane took me to the Hospital Auxiliary's Bazaar Extravaganza. A flea market to beat all others! The Auxiliary told Jane that I could pick out whatever I needed for my apartment. By the end of that day, you would not believe the stuff Jane and I had gathered. Other community folks quickly filled the gap with what we didn't find. My newly-furnished apartment was filled with things that made me realize that this was going to be home.

I moved into my new home in December. My first night was filled with excitement and downright fear! If I could just make the first night, I knew there would be nothing I couldn't handle. It took four months to get the extra necessary paid help I needed to maintain living in my new home. In the meantime, my support circle became attendant care workers for my evening care. Each person from my support circle took turns coming in and helping me into my bed at night. Unbelievable!

Members of my circle caught wind that people who lived in my apartment building did not like the idea of me living there. They were concerned that the building would turn into a nursing home. My friend Jane, and her Lioness friends, decided to host a house-warming party at my place and invited everyone in the building. It was a smashing success. Not only did the tenants turn out in full force, but some of the hospital staff came as well, with welcoming gifts.

That first year was something to remember.

As I look back on my accomplishments, I feel so proud of myself. I can't thank my support circle enough for what they did for me.

However, even after that first year, a big part of my life was still missing. It was my family.

I showed my unhappiness not by words but through my actions. I became more withdrawn and had no desire to go anywhere. Sometimes, you don't even know what the root of your unhappiness is until someone helps you figure it out.

Diane and I both remember the day I wheeled myself into her office and she asked me why I looked so down. As soon as she asked me, my eyes filled up with tears and I said, " How can I get to see my boys more often?"

You see, I was unsure of my relationship with Raymond and Steven and I was scared of pushing them away. I did not have the courage to ask the boys to stay with me in fear of what they would say. I needed some help to ask. Diane offered. It seemed like a simple thing she did. She asked the boys if they wanted to spend a weekend here with me. They both agreed and thought it was a great idea.

That Saturday, in November, was the beginning of our family reunion. As a matter of fact, we had Christmas together for the first time in 10 years.

There is nothing in this world that is more important than my children. I really believe that without my support circle, I would not have my family back.

Steven and Raymond spend entire weekends, holidays and summer vacations with me. I love them so much! I once had attendant care workers come every night to put me to bed. Now, Steven and Raymond do that when they are with me. Things are so different from the days when I lived in the hospital. How scared and nervous the boys must have been when they came to visit me there!

I once believed other people knew what was best for me. Now I know what is best for myself and I like it that way. I still have many fears like everyone else, but the fears, that I once had are not important anymore. I have new challenges today and isn't that what life is all about!

Thank a for believing in me.

Brenda

*I had only been with the family for a few hours, but it was quickly obvious to me how lucky they were to have each other. The atmosphere was light as they joked, teased, laughed and shared their memories of growing up together.*

*In talking with Brian's support worker, Ruth, later that night, she told me that every time she talks with Brian, he never misses saying, "Pete. Always my brother, always my brother."*

*Brian's brother, Pete, tells the family story.*

*I*t had been a cold, blustery Halloween night. Early the following morning, the house was very still as everyone slept. Everyone except Brian. He crept quietly down the stairs without waking anyone. He found the keys to our brother Lorne's bright yellow Dart Swinger that had black racing stripes. Brian somehow got the car to go in reverse. The car swung around, smacked into a fencepost and roughed up the fender. Brian went back into the house, put the keys back exactly where he found them and went back to bed.

You can imagine the reaction of Lorne when he discovered his new car all smashed up! We all thought this must have been a Halloween prank. Brian did not exactly volunteer information at first. Some time later that day, he finally owned up to it.

It was clear to us as his brothers and sisters, that Brian was constantly trying to be just like us. He certainly proved it that morning. Especially when Lorne wanted to strangle him like he would any one of us who had damaged his pride and joy!

I remember when Brian was born. Mom and Dad could have put him into a facility but they refused. We had a neighbour who sent their son to a facility. This neighbour would bug Mom constantly and tell her that she should do the same. There was no way in the world Mom would ever consider it.

Mom was extremely protective of Brian and whatever Brian wanted, Brian got. My sister, Linda and I did all the disciplining. Mom never did. It was too hard for her. It was like her guilt overpowered her and she couldn't give Brian heck for anything.

When Brian kept on saying he wanted his own place, Mom helped him set up his own place downstairs in their home. She struggled with Brian leaving, but knew she should plan for his future. Although her heart told her differently, she put Brian on a waiting list for a children's group home. When Brian was 15 years old, he did leave home because a space became available. It was a brand new building and about 40 kids lived there.

It was a terrible, terrible year, certainly the worst year ever for all of us. They told Mom and Dad that they didn't want to send Brian home on weekends because they could not handle him when he returned to the group home. Mom and Dad insisted and Brian did continue to come home on weekends. Linda and her friend, Lori Lee (who by the way is my wife now!) would have to take Brian back because Mom could not bear the pain of leaving him. Linda and Lori Lee were only 16 years old at the time. It took all they had to leave him there.

Brian would run away from this place. One time the police brought him home in the cruiser because he tried to hitch-hike home. The only problem was he was going in the wrong direction. I remember Dad saying, "Let's not call them and tell them Brian is here. Let's see how long it will take them to realize that Brian is missing." He was there hours before the group home finally contacted Mom and Dad. It is no wonder after that awful year, Mom never wanted to see Brian leave home.

But Brian was insistent that he wanted his own apartment. Eventually, Mom knew she had to let go but it was too tough for her to make that decision alone. We knew she needed us to help her through this one. I know at first she thought we were the bad guys.

We had a big meeting where the local association and our family got together. We all got to ask questions and talk about our fears. Again, Linda and I had to steer Mom in the right direction. I knew Brian was capable of so much more. I treated him like the rest of my brothers and expected the same from him. Fear - yes, but I never had any doubt. Although we believed in Brian, we were all scared.

When he got his first apartment, it was right down the street from Mom and Dad. This was helpful because Mom could still watch him like a hawk!

Mom's health took a turn for the worse. She passed away within a short time of Brian leaving the nest. We are so glad that she left our world with peace of mind knowing Brian was doing great.

Brian has no doubt proven to the world what he was trying to tell us for so long. He finally left the workshop which he had wanted to do for a long time. He now has a full-time job at a local factory and he makes over $9.00 an hour. We are very proud of him. At work, Brian won a "Golden Broom Award". This award is given to only one person out of all the employees at 25 warehouses. Brian earned that award.

Every Saturday morning, I wait to hear the phone ring. I know it will be Brian. Once again, we will have to decide whose turn it is to buy the coffee. Then off we go, Brian, myself, my son Matt and my daughter, Amelia. We will always be a close family.

*Personal mementoes in an office are often pretty and can carry a message. When I remarked on a brightly coloured butterfly adorning Helen's office, I had no idea how much it represented. To Helen, this butterfly is a symbol of great change, growth and a beautiful experience. This is her story of how people who explored a vision together ended up becoming closer to each other than they had ever imagined. A family is the people involved who bring the dignity, care and respect that are shared and expressed among its members. Gently, Helen reflects a story of such a family.*

At Shirley's birthday party, we all knew that our dream could come true. Shirley and her sisters were sitting around the kitchen table eating cake: a family had been born. A group of people committed to finding a family for Shirley had become one.

We started with people from the Friendship Club, the church, and staff from the group home where Shirley was living. We worked together to map out a future with Shirley. As dreams of the group grew, the differences between agency and family became pronounced. The people who were later to become like older sisters to Shirley drew up a covenant of their shared responsibilities. The covenant defined the role of the agency and the obligations of Shirley's family.

The group met frequently. It wasn't easy to develop a plan, and we learned together. Plans became the dream of the whole family.

Audrey, Anne, Ann, Janet and Shirley were like sisters growing closer to each other over the years. They grew to love each other dearly. I could feel it in the tenderness expressed among the women and in the way they talked with each other. There was a sense that nothing would separate them.

By the time of the birthday, Anne and her husband Andy, had made a commitment to Shirley. They would sell their farm, and buy a house that was wheelchair accessible.

Shirley was to have her own private space which included her bedroom, and a place to entertain guests. Everything was in place and ready to go. This was all about to happen. It only needed to be physically carried out.

At one point, we were discussing concerns about health, as Shirley was spending more and more time in hospital. The year before, Shirley had been admitted one or two times, and this year was being admitted more often. Then the agency called to tell us that another group home had a space open for Shirley, but there must be an answer given immediately. Shirley did not have a lot of control over her body, but she literally leapt out of her chair at this, even with her safety strap on. Shirley clearly rejected this proposition. She wanted to live with Anne and Andy. There was no question that living with her family was the most important thing to her.

I could sit in a room with Shirley and feel her message. Her smile was the only recognizable form of communication to many. She couldn't move for herself, or talk. She showed disdain by rolling her eyes upward. Shirley resonated with a strong sense of Peace. That was why people fell in love with both Shirley and each other. She attracted people who really cared and drew these people in closer to her and to each other. She radiated power in a room. If people were open enough to feel it, they could become part of it. Shirley understood everything we said. It is only our lack of understanding, lack of thinking creatively or not listening to our intuition that hold us apart. Shirley talked all the time, she just didn't use spoken language. Shirley chose her friends and relegated those who did not recognize her to some other place. No one in her family questioned that Shirley was part of the conversation. You simply knew that she knew.

We were helped by Shirley's strength. When there were problems, like when Anne and Andy's farm didn't sell, we needed to go on and make new plans. The disappointment turned into an idea to adapt the farmhouse. We happily made plans to change the laundry room, knock out walls and build a ramp. A group of men from Shirley's church were eager to help.

We had talked about problems of transportation. Shirley couldn't sit safely in a car seat even with a safety belt. If we could get an old van with a lift, the church offered to keep it in running condition. It was their contribution to a fellow member. Shirley and her friends celebrated each achievement.

We were excited that parts of the dream were falling into place. The group had written down their expectations and was in the process of carrying those out. There was a sense of completion, of having done what we set out to do. Shirley's intention was to have a family and she had found one. It proved to me that it doesn't matter whether you live with a biological family or whether you choose your family. It is important that you are loved and give love.

Shirley died as the dream was about to happen. If things had come together easily and quickly, Shirley may not have gained a family. The struggle actually energized people and brought them together in commitment and love. It accentuated people's gifts throughout both the conflicts and the solutions.

It was sad when she died. She was twenty-four and all her lifelong possessions were gathered together into two cardboard boxes. Many of Shirley's precious possessions were gifts from other people. As mementoes, gifts given to Shirley were returned. In this way, the memory was given back to family and friends. Treasured moments could now be relived: the reason for buying the present, the time and place of giving, and Shirley's delight in the gift.

I was given a photograph, and a butterfly Shirley and a friend had made. I can only guess that it might mean breaking out of a cocoon and flying free after the long struggle.

# *listening to each other*

*T*alking is a link between people. This form of communication is used most often to learn about one another, and build relationships. When people do not use spoken language to express themselves, we must take notice of how they do communicate, and perhaps learn new ways of conversing with them.

There are many ways people can tell their stories. Some people communicate with sign language, others use letter boards, and still others communicate through art work. We also need to be sensitive to the nuance of a smile, or a frown, to hand movements, or to shrugged shoulders. When we put this information together, we can usually hear what it is people have to say, and learn more about what it is they want us to know about themselves.

*The search for God is a very personal journey. For Dalton, spirituality has been a very significant part of his life. But it has only been in the three years since being welcomed to one of the L'Arche Christian Communities, that people close to him saw his spirituality and helped him nurture it. Up until then, Dalton had spent 15 years in a nursing home bed.*

*Dalton doesn't use spoken language to communicate. Until a year and a half ago, his primary means of communication was body language.*

*It was then Dalton first got a communication board. It was simple - a series of symbols and words. Within two months Dalton knew 30 symbols and was using three word phrases. He was also putting symbols together to create words that weren't yet part of his symbol board. Like the day he told his workers about his "church family". He had been confirmed in his church that weekend. Or when he repeatedly pointed to the combination of "Easter" and "Book". You see, there was no symbol on his board for "Bible".*

*I*t's a sunny day. Dalton and I meet in a room with a big window. I'm glad because I need to look out every now and then to take a deep breath. Dalton amazes me.

I had spoken to Dalton a few days before about getting together to talk about his life. He seemed excited at the time, but I didn't know if my questions would be too personal.

Dalton and Marg are waiting. Marg, the facilitator, holds Dalton's hand so only his thumb and first finger are free. The Letter Board sits within reach of Dalton. He answers the questions by pointing to the letters and spelling words.

After each letter, Marg pulls his hand back. She reminds Dalton to be accurate. Dalton is so anxious to answer some of the questions that he bangs the board passionately.

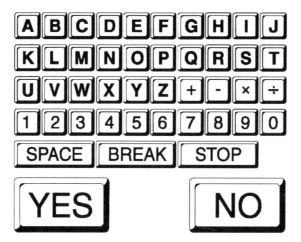

It's hard to imagine this man spending years in a nursing home bed. I start my questions by asking him about his time at the nursing home.

*Did you spend any time out of bed, Dalton?*

*How did you feel when you lived there?*

Others have also followed Dalton. Former staff of the nursing home still keep in touch with Dalton and occasionally visit.

*How do you feel about your life now, Dalton?*

. After these opening questions, we move easily into conversation. Knowing that Dalton's spirituality is important to him, I know where to start.

*What does God mean to you, Dalton?*

I tell Dalton that if my questions are too personal, to point to the [ STOP ] symbol on the board. But Dalton has been closed up for too long and is anxious to express his feelings.

*What do you pray for?*

*Peace for who?*

*Do you pray for anything for yourself?*

We take a few breaks because it's physically, and I suspect, emotionally tiring for Dalton. After an hour, Dalton looks drained. I'm drained.

I ask Dalton who he would like me to talk to about his story. He uses his book of pictures to point to Laurie.

When I meet Laurie, I can't get my pen out fast enough or keep up with her. What her words don't say, her eyes do. She is sharing her spiritual journey with Dalton as Dalton shares his with her.

Laurie and Dalton have been going to church together for three years. They sit together near the front where a pew has been modified to accommodate Dalton's wheelchair. "What is so wonderful is the truthfulness of his expression, the passion, life, and energy that comes from him so spontaneously. He laughs and calls out, and at the end of the sermon will shout, 'Yeah!' and laugh. During the intercessory prayers, he raises both his hands on each 'Amen', like the fist in the 'right on' gesture. He helps me express myself, I want to shout out too. It's such a bond we have, as if we are one person experiencing the same emotions. It's very genuine and natural. Some people might be uncomfortable with his expressiveness, but is it right to suppress it and have him sit there looking bored?"

Dalton and Laurie have been through many issues together at church. As Laurie says, "He has caused so much turmoil of the best kind!" Dalton's demonstrative and affectionate nature is welcomed and respected as he and the Minister hug after communion. But the question has been raised as to whether or not this is standing in the way of the congregation seeing Dalton as an adult and not as a child. Laurie says, "We can learn a lot from Dalton about honesty of emotion and expression, and we need to see that capacity in ourselves."

Dalton's spirituality has been nurtured both at home and at church. His Minister has been a vital part of Dalton's growth. Dalton reached out to him by using his symbol board to say:

*You have questions about God, Dalton?*

*Who do you want to visit?*

*Why do you want to visit your Minister?*

Dalton's presence has done more than help create visible changes. John, the Minister, is very moved by Dalton's contribution to the life of the Church. "He has taught me more in three years than I have taught him. He's made us more aware of the L'Arche Community. He's made us blatantly aware that someone whom we would perceive to be so handicapped has a spiritual awareness and centre that would make an average parishioner blush." John also jokes that Dalton is the only fellow who makes a comment at the end of the sermons by yelling, "Yeah!"

John says, "Dalton is sensitizing us to people with special needs, but at the same time is desensitizing us in terms of our own prejudices. Our perceptions get in the way. Out of our needs, we think they have no intellectual capability, no spiritual centre. He's made us aware of how wrong we were."

*Dalton, what do you talk to God about?*

Dalton and his father, Jim, see each other every couple of weeks. Jim too has seen changes in Dalton. "He has more confidence. He's learning, and learning fast. You've got to expect things out of people and help them do it. That's not just Dalton. That's everybody, as far as I'm concerned. Bring everybody out more and more and make the world a better place."

*Dalton, when people read this book, what do you want them to know about you?*

The day after our talk, Marg asked Dalton how he felt about it.

When asked why he felt good, Dalton said,

*I knocked on the door. No response. I banged on the glass. No answer. I searched for the bell. No luck. I checked my watch... oops, I had forgotten my watch. Was it the right time? Had our appointment been forgotten? Then I remembered the instructions given to me by the person who interpreted on the phone. If there is no answer, just go in and find him. He will be expecting you.*

*In I went and down to Frank's domain. I banged loudly on his door and stomped my feet. I would have flicked the light switch if I could have found one. The door burst open and Frank welcomed me, clearly pleased that I had found him. After showing me a chair where I could sit, he reminded me in sign language that we had met once before.*

*A poster on the wall then caught his eye and he pointed out Dave Winfield, the baseball player, as his hero. As I glanced around the room it became apparent that people were important to Frank. As I asked about one particular picture on the bookshelf, a story unfolded.*

*T*his is my mother and father and me in the middle. We lived on a farm with land all around. I would cut the grass (wipes imaginary sweat off his brow) and work hard. This is my twin brother (pointing to a wedding picture). He works with wood. I have two sisters. One works with her husband (pointing to another family picture) and builds. My sister in this picture lives in British Columbia with her family. I have visited her three times for vacation. The last time I went alone. I was a little nervous, but I loved the plane ride.

We heard a noise and Frank opened the door. His parents had come to visit. Joining the conversation where we had left off, Frank's parents added that the sense of independence he gained from making the trip alone was very important. "When he was born, the doctor said Frank would never walk, or talk or ever hear. It was not a very hopeful prognosis at a time when we were busy with two small babies, one in each arm to hold."

Born at the same time, the twins were given such a different forecast for their future. Years later, the doctor met Frank again. According to Frank's mother, the doctor's eyes bulged out and his jaw dropped open with surprise.

Frank walks with a limp, but moves with healthy energy. He does not have mobility with his one arm, but compensates for it by using his other arm, face and upper body to communicate. With a hearing aid, Frank can hear a little. He has learned to read lips and to say some words. With his family's love, he has achieved more than anyone had ever predicted at his birth.

As with most deaf students attending a residential school, Frank left his family during the week, but he was able to come home on weekends. Frank enjoyed math especially, but his reading and spelling skills were weak. It was a shock when the school phoned one day to say Frank would soon be finished school. When you reach a certain age, you cannot continue. But where was Frank to go?

"It was a dreadful time for everyone," says Frank's mother. "The deaf said he was handicapped and the handicapped said he was deaf. Frank did not seem to fit in anywhere. It was very frustrating." That was the feeling the family was left with after approaching different people seeking some direction and assistance for Frank. For months after leaving school, Frank sat around at home on the farm growing more and more depressed. Neither he nor his family knew which way to turn. Finally, Frank entered the local workshop despite feeling this was not the place for him.

Finding a job was still one of Frank's goals and one day an opening came up in a local plant. The management at the plant was interested in someone who could work an afternoon shift unsupervised. Frank was eager to apply for this position, undaunted by all the possible obstacles.

The interview was not a typical one. The central question was whether he could prove he had the physical strength to do the job. Frank was shown how to use the equipment, and was told that he would be expected to wash at least a couple of trucks per hour. An audience gathered to watch him try. Frank's support worker was there and acted as an interpreter. She recalled, "There must have been ten people there to watch Frank wash a truck!" After about thirty minutes, Frank had washed five trucks. Frank's comment was that if the washer hose had an extra handle on it, it would work even better for him. By the next day, the boss had an extra handle right where Frank had suggested. No one questioned Frank's ability to wash trucks after that.

For the first two weeks, Frank had his support worker with him. At one point, one of the men asked, "He's not going to leave us is he?" concerned that this was only a 'work placement' for Frank. After the co-workers learned some sign language, the support worker reduced her visits. By now, hand signals and gestures were being used to pass on praise, give instruction and tell jokes.

"He is a regular guy here," says Jim. Another co-worker, Flemming says, "Frank is a good guy. He is willing to do anything. If you need help, he doesn't just stand there and look. He helps without having to be asked." One of Flemming's stories about Frank involves a plugged vacuum hose. It seems that Flemming was at a loss as to how to unplug it until Frank grabbed the broom and motioned for Flemming to go up the ladder. Frank gestured for Flemming to push the broom handle down to unplug the clog. "I never even thought of doing that," laughs Flemming.

When asked about his job, Frank's face lights up into a huge grin. He signs that sometimes they have water fights or snowball fights at work for fun. Frank has acquired a reputation for his practical jokes.

Frank's brother, John recently had his truck painted with his name on it to promote his construction business. A woman came up and asked if he was Frank's brother. John thought that was a little odd, but when two more people came up to ask if he was related to Frank, he began to realize how popular Frank had become. "Maybe I should have painted, 'I'm Frank's brother', on the truck. It might have been better advertising!"

*I am an artist. And I live with my parents. Art has been my favourite hobby for a long time. I entered some of the pictures at the fair. After a few years I decided to take art classes to improve my painting. My friend Jean teaches me acrylic. I go to the Artist Workshop classes too. My pictures were adding up so I sold most of them at an Art Show.*

*I also sold some pictures at the Farmers' Market. I did not like to be left alone, so volunteers helped me set up my display, write out bills and make change. I liked meeting people, but my art was not selling, so I decided not to go anymore. A local Member of Parliament said he would have a private show of my art. I was very nervous at first, but I ended up enjoying the show.*

*I enjoy my art. It makes me feel good. I am very proud of my "Duck in Flight".*

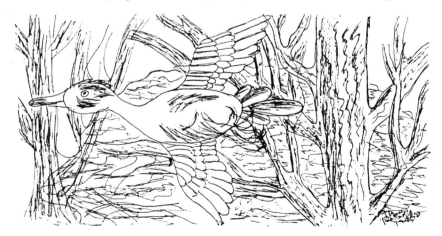

# point of light

$A$ point of light ignites within when we start believing in ourselves. Whether it's a flicker or a full beam of light, there are always challenges to overcome. It becomes easier when others start believing in us as well.

When that happens, we discover ways in which we want to give and receive. We contribute.

Contributing may include our volunteer work, giving to family life, having a job, joining social groups, developing spirituality, or pursuing further education. As the following stories show, there are many opportunities to develop and share our point of light.

# *A Letter From Paul*

To all who helped me,

My dreams have come true. I met Brenda, who is the most beautiful girl in town. I have my own business. I have God who gives me strength to get through each day. For all this, I thank the people who have been part of making this happen. But first, let me tell what has happened in my life so far.

Six months after I was born, the family was driving home from the cottage. There was a car accident and the Lord took my parents home to Him. I had brain-damage and my left arm had paralysis. I grew up in foster homes and helped on farms. I went to public school and finished the two-year program at high school. I think it helps to have an education. After completing school, I knew I couldn't handle the pace of a factory job, but what could I do? I knew what hard work was. I had worked on the farm and you had to work hard there.

I moved to live in a group home and then, months later, to an apartment with a roommate. I started at the workshop in town. I worked in the lawn maintenance program and I liked the work. Ever since I was a young boy, I liked the outdoors and I liked to keep busy. But I knew I could get more money by working outside the workshop. I left the workshop and I started to work on a poultry farm. I had completed two years of work, when one day, as I moved the gutter cleaner, I hurt my back. I had to stop working while my back healed.

By this time, the lawn care had faded out as part of the workshop contracts. I decided I would start my own business of lawn care and snow removal. In summer I would ride my bike from job to job, pulling the push mower behind me. Then I bought a weedeater which meant I would have to make two trips. I needed it to make the work look good, but it took a little longer and it was hot and sweaty.

If it wasn't for Brian, my support worker, I would still be working that way. He gave me a copy of Farm Auto Trader and suggested I could buy a tractor. He let me decide for myself. It's true that when I did the work the old-fashioned way by hand, I would come home grumpy and tired. I had blisters on my hands and once I pinched a nerve in my shoulder. I decided to buy the tractor and that meant I had to spend all my savings, but now I can put a blade on the front or carry a snowblower in the winter.

Thanks to that good idea, my work is easier and I can get more done.

Sometimes it's easy, but sometimes it's hard. It costs money to keep a business going, and I need to keep enough money saved for repairs. I don't spend money I don't have. I keep track of my expenses and the money I earn so I can pay my taxes. You can't cheat the government!

It is worth it to have your own business. I recommend it. It doesn't have to be lawn care. It can be any goal. You should try to achieve it; it just takes reasonable rates and hard work. The businesses around town are opening their doors to let all the people in. In the winter, I shovel and scrape for lawyers, an optometrist, a chiropractor and seniors. I know whose sidewalks I have to have cleaned off before 8:00 a.m., and whose can wait a little. I can't do them all at once. Sometimes it's hard to get up out of bed at all. I don't always have the ambition. I have to work at it and coax myself to get out of bed. The business is very important to me, and my customers come first. After all, that's how I get more customers, by word of mouth. I want people to be happy with my work.

I am happy in my life. I have to take it easier and slow down a little. Everyone says I work too hard and that I never stop to rest. I married a year ago and my wife Brenda will help me with that. The Good Lord will watch over me and the Pastor and his wife visit us often. Brenda and I are active in the Church. We also help with the Friendship Club on Tuesday night. Brian comes over to see if he can help us in any way.

I am thankful to all the people that have helped me along the way. I could not have done it without you. I am blessed. I can do everything, perhaps at a different pace, than other people. God gives us health and strength to get through our daily work. A special thank you to my beautiful wife, Brenda. I love you.

Sincerely,

Paul

# *A Letter To Paul*

Dear Paul,

It makes me happy that my family accepts you as one of them. I know when I first came to this foster family, I didn't know what to call them. Now we both call them Mom and Dad. My new family has taught me right from wrong and gave me love and affection over the years. I am very grateful to my mom for all her understanding. All the family treats me like a real sister.

You know I was born with spina bifida. I didn't tell you that the doctors said I might never talk or walk, and that I would spend my life in a bed. I lived in an institution for years, and then with my family, but to be here in our own place with you is a miracle. To finally be married and in our own apartment is wonderful.

I remember when we worked at the workshop. If I wasn't at the shop on time, they would give me a good talking to. It's hard to walk any distance, for me, and I know I can't go as fast as the rest of the world. Now to be able to work at the library downtown is great. I can't reach the high spots, but I clean windows, vacuum and do inventory as best I can. My boss accepts me as a worker. I know I am growing, not on the outside, but on the inside. That is important to me.

You help me when I get scared. Like the time I went to the high school to talk to the class about handicaps. I was so scared at first because I didn't know how they would react. I have been hurt by people who call me names or make fun of me. I took a big breath and looked at the class. Then I said, I've got something to tell you. And they listened. I told them how I used to come home crying because I did not feel welcome. I told them how today it is changing and I brag about you.

I taught you how to laugh and not be so serious. You taught me how to belong in a couple.

I love you,

Brenda

# *A Letter To Paul*

Paul,

When I tell people you are a remarkable man, I mean it. Your customers say it best. They say the competition doesn't do, "near as good a job", as you do. I know you are so busy in the summer that you have had to turn customers away.

Joan, a long time customer, says you are "always a pleasure" and will be cutting their lawn for as long as you want to. She says, "He does a good job and I don't have to worry if I'm home or away. No complaints at all!" Bill, Joan's husband, agrees. "Paul, to me, is a great guy and you can trust him with anything. I'm happy with Paul and happy with his work. I've got no beefs at all."

Paul has had his grass cut for three years now. He says he heard about your good reputation around town. "Everybody knows him," he says. "He'll be cutting my grass for as long as I'm here."

Pat, who has been your customer for years, is happy with the professional job you do on her lawn. Pat says, "You've got to give people a chance. And if a few more people were given a break, it would be a lot better! Just because people have a physical handicap or a mental handicap doesn't mean that they can't do the job well."

It's not hard to understand why your customers speak so highly of you and your work, Paul. You think of your customers first and work hard. The prices are fair and you keep good records in your account book. Keep up the good work and remember to take a vacation!

All the best,

Brian

*It was very inspiring to be sitting in Marg's living room surrounded by her close family members. I was touched by their sensitivity in helping Marg tell her story. They wanted to give without taking away. This story reflects Marg's words as well as her family's.*

*As our time together went on, I could hear Marg wanting to share more and more of herself. Several times she exclaimed, "Put that part in my story!"*

The first day of high school, I got on the wrong bus to go home. For what seemed like hours, I sat on the bus as it went around and around the city. I could not tell time, but I knew after watching so many people get on and get off the bus that something was wrong. Finally the driver noticed I was still there. It was pitch dark and I knew Mom would be upset and maybe call the cops.

As soon as he said, "I bet you got on the wrong bus," I burst into tears. He drove me home. I ran into the house as fast as I could, crying and shaking. I was hysterical. My mom said, "You are not going back." That was my first and my last day of high school.

I stayed with my mom at home for years and years. I never went anywhere. Plus, I would not even answer the door. I watched TV and helped my mom out. My biggest problem was that I ate all the time. I became very overweight. The only winter coat I had was this big white coat. I remember one day someone yelled at me, "Hey, you great white whale!" I could have died. It hurt so much.

My mom became very sick. My brothers and sisters were there as much as they could be, but they relied on me to help Mom. The nurse actually trained me to do things for Mom as she became weaker. I helped her with bathing, changing her colostomy bag, and packing her open sores with bandages.

When Mom finally had to go into the hospital, I would sit with her everyday. She slept most of the time, but I was there in case she woke up and needed something. I sat with her for six months.

Mom died and I was so sad. The rest of the family were sad too. We had a big family meeting because we could not afford to keep the house. Nine people sat around the kitchen table trying to come up with ideas.

Everyone thought I would live with one of my brothers or sisters. I will never forget blurting out the words, "I want to live on my own!" There was dead silence.

Then I heard someone say, "Let's go for it, Marg!" We all agreed. My family had heard of a woman named Ruth who was a good support worker. We called the local Association for Community Living to see if Ruth would help me get an apartment.

Ruth also helped me find a weight loss clinic. I was so overweight. At the time, I weighed 360 pounds. Slowly, slowly I began to take off my weight. It has been a long two years of hard work, but today I am 200 pounds lighter! I know my mom would be so proud of me today. Ruth still helps me to keep on track. I can't read, so Ruth and I use pictures to plan out my meals so I know what to eat each day.

These days, my brother Mike tells me the only problem is trying to find me at home. Then he says, "Oh, it's the kind of problem we are glad to have, Marg!" I guess he was kidding me. But it's true, because I'm so busy now. It beats watching TV all day.

One of my favourite things is to go shopping. I don't have to shop at only certain stores anymore to find clothes that fit. Now I can go to any store. I love all the clothes. Dressing up is wonderful, especially when I go dancing. It's great to let my hair down!

Ruth helped me find volunteer work with little children. I play with the kids, wash the toys and some days, join in the craft class with the moms and dads. I knit too. I like to knit so much that I knit over a hundred pairs of slippers each year for needy people.

I've met some nice people at the bowling alley. A lady named Betty told me she knew my mom years ago. The next time I saw her, she brought in old pictures of my mom and her when they were younger. I have fun bowling with my new friends.

I go to church every Sunday. My friends Kay and Jack used to pick me up. After church, we would go out for tea, toast and juice. Jack died, but Kay and I still call each other every now and then.

I have more friends. One of my friends is an older lady who I see once a week. I make her tea and we visit. Plus, Brenda and Rick call me and ask if I can babysit their six-year-old daughter. I love Ashley. When I had to have an operation a year ago, I was so surprised and happy when the whole family visited me in the hospital.

I still have pictures of when I weighed 360 pounds. I burned the big white winter coat, the coat that I wore when people called me "white whale". I keep those pictures to remind me how great I feel today and how happy I am to be doing so much. If I want to speak my mind, I will speak it. I once relied on my family to speak for me. Gee, I love my brothers and sisters! Even though I don't always listen to them, I know they are so proud of me and like hearing me speak for myself.

Things have changed since my first day of high school when I got on the wrong bus. Now I know the city so well and people ask me which would be the best bus route to take!

Theresa
DeSerrano
1993

*It's hard to believe that a snapshot taken of Stephen, 15 years ago, portrayed a shy, awkward little boy. The day I met him, energy, life and genuine excitement poured out.*

*Stephen's mother and father tell us why that snapshot showed such a different child.*

*Stephen told me why his picture has changed.*

*His parents and Stephen himself want to tell their own stories. Each story could stand on its own, and yet, neither could be separate from the other.*

At a very early age, we realized that Stephen was not doing what we thought a normal kid should be doing, at least according to Dr. Spock. When Stephen was two years old, he had so much difficulty holding things and he tripped constantly. Things were not quite right. The specialist thought he would grow out of it. We waited and hoped.

Those first years of Stephen's life were an emotional roller coaster for our family. How could our only son have so many problems?

Finally, the doctor sent Stephen to the hospital for a series of tests. We will never forget that day. His morning was filled with blood tests and brain scans. You name it, he had it. By the afternoon, he didn't know what was coming next. He entered the hearing room for further tests and was frightened by the ear phones. As he tried to pull the ear phones away, the assistant slapped his hands. No wonder Stephen remained shy over the years and continued to have difficulty expressing his feelings.

We had a hard time accepting the labels put on him. Like many other parents, we wanted to believe none of this was true. We have come to realize that every family goes through happy and not so happy moments in their lives.

We have always considered ourselves an ordinary family trying to do our best.

Stephen attended a regular pre-school. He went to a public school for a short time before he was placed into a segregated school. We decided to move away from the big city to a smaller community to raise our children. We felt that Stephen had attended a segregated school long enough and we wanted him to have the chance to go to the same school as his sister Sandra.

It was our family dream.

After searching for the right home, we moved into a house that was located one block away from the school. We looked into whether this school had a special education class for Stephen's age; it did. It appeared to us that our family dream of both children walking to school together was about to come true. We met with the school board and plans were set in motion for this to happen. We were all excited. And then we received a phone call.

During the summer months, the school board had changed their mind. They told us that they thought Stephen would do better at another school where there were smaller children - kindergarten age. They said that it was better for Stephen to excel rather than risk the chance of failure. Stephen was squashed. So was Sandra.

As the old saying goes, "Hindsight is 20/20." We knew our son better than anyone. But we allowed other people to tell us what was best. As parents, we felt too intimidated to challenge their decision, so Stephen was bussed away to another school in another community. We felt that it was an entire year wasted.

We will never forget watching Stephen stand in front of the neighbourhood school, waiting for the bus that took him away. The children with whom he attended school were six or seven and Stephen was 13! We remember Stephen saying, "They are not even as tall as me!"

Sometimes it takes so much energy to fight for what is important to you. Stephen and Sandra are worth fighting for, no matter what the cost. The following year, things changed. We finally convinced the school board that Stephen should go to our neighbourhood school. That was a turning point. For Stephen and our family, there was no looking back.

The experience with the education system, years ago, has made us stronger today.

We thank people like Trish, who, as a support worker, helped us through some very tough times. She came to us when we needed help. She cared. When it was convenient for our family to gather, Trish would give up her Sunday afternoons to meet with us.

We have learned that there are people who believe in people, and then there are those who get caught in the system. We have grown to realize what kind of service we want. It is one that helps us, as parents, understand things without making us feel guilty. Also, it encourages us to take an active part in getting what we need for our children.

There have been people who have done just that. They have made us feel so comfortable we could open up and talk. You get to know the people you can trust. Stephen will tell you that too.

*Stephen did tell me, as he and his family related his story.*

I had one year of high school left. We moved again. I could have been bussed back to that same school but my family and I decided no more bussing. I stayed at home for a whole year. Even though I helped out a lot with the clean up of our new home, which had five acres of land, I was bored.

My sister was volunteering in town. Through her connections, she heard that there was an association that might help me out. Trish was the first person we met. She took Mom, Dad and me on a tour of the sheltered workshop. I was so scared! People came up and hugged me, and I didn't even know who they were! I wanted to get away from there.

Trish asked me what I was interested in doing. She kept on saying that the only thing that was important was what "I" wanted to do. I told her that I had lots of work experiences when I was at high school. My favourite job was working at a pre-school nursery.

Within a short time, Trish helped me get a volunteer position at a local nursery school working with the kids and in the kitchen. For the next two years, I left my home at 7:00 a.m. and worked all day long at the nursery school.

I was very comfortable there. It took time for me to realize that I did a lot for the school. So much, that I began to think I should get paid for the work I did. The chef, who I worked with in the kitchen, went to the nursery school's Board of Directors monthly meeting. He told them how important my work was and suggested that I should get paid. A short time after that, he died. The Board's decision was that they did not have any money to pay me.

I tried a part-time job at a fast food restaurant that paid me money. There was only one problem, I wasn't "fast" enough. I dropped burgers, I spilled pop, I ran around like a chicken with its head cut off. I hated it! At the same time, I continued to help out at the nursery school.

With the help of an employment support worker, I got a full-time job that I could handle at a family restaurant. I have worked there for two years. I have never called in sick and work a full 40 hour week. I like it there and I think they like me.

I did ask to get some Saturdays off in the past. This was so I could go with my Grandma to the symphony orchestra performances. Grandma taught me to like music. Grandma passed away not too long ago and I still miss her very much. I remember the day Mom and Dad told me that she had died, I felt so empty.

We had a major family crisis right after I started working at my new job. Dad went on strike. Two weeks before Dad went on strike, Sandra got married. One week after that, Mom hurt her back and could not work. Mom and Dad drained their bank account to pay for Sandra's wedding. I am sure they would do the same all over again if they had to. I am sure they do not regret it one bit.

I had to bring home the "dough". There were days when I felt pressured. I would say things to Mom and Dad that probably hurt them like, "Why don't you go back to work?"

That was yesterday and we got through it all. Once Dad got back to work, he had the chance to go to Japan for nine weeks for work training. Grandma had passed away and Sandra was no longer living at home. I decided to move into my own apartment. I am sure Mom went through a very difficult time. She told me that she was not sure if she was doing the right thing. One day, I overheard her say to a friend, "How do we know that we're not throwing Stephen out into the wild!" But despite her own fears, she kept on going and helped me move in.

Today, I live in my own apartment which is walking distance from my job. I have neighbours who come for tea and I go to their homes. I still go to Mom and Dad's on the weekends. Mom likes to do my laundry. Someday I am sure she is going to wonder why she is still doing it. I will keep bringing it until she figures that out!

One of the highlights in my life was going to England and Scotland with Mom and Dad last year. I got the chance to see where they were born.

I still dream of getting a paid job at a nursery school. I am a leader for a Beaver Colony and volunteer once a week. I have many friends who volunteer on the same night. It feels good when the little kids run up to me and talk to me and ask for some help. Kids are neat.

I am not "special" any more. I think I have been able to drop the label. I don't go to a "special" school or work at a "special" workplace or live in any "special" home. I am just an ordinary guy, living an ordinary life, filled with ups and downs. It is great!

*Gord is a volunteer. The people who know him enjoy talking about the difference volunteering has made in his life. Gord didn't answer many of my questions with words, but he showed his enthusiasm about his volunteer experience, at the museum, with a grin.*

*Katherine is the Volunteer Coordinator at the museum. In describing Gord as a volunteer, she simply takes her hands and indicates a flower blooming. She appreciates his contribution. That's why she nominated Gord, above 95 other volunteers, for a Provincial Outstanding Achievement Award. She relates the story.*

*I* felt somewhat apprehensive about having adults who are developmentally challenged volunteer at our museum site. This would be a new experience for all of us and my fear was that it wouldn't work out. After getting the full support from my colleagues to welcome and support the new volunteers, the placement began two years ago on a trial basis. When the volunteers first came out, I noted one fellow in particular by the name of Gord, who was painfully shy. He hung his head most of the time and avoided eye contact. Was he as nervous as I was about all this? Possibly. Was he picking up on my tension? Probably. Whatever Gord or the other volunteers may have been feeling, whatever the need for distance might have been, my acceptance was unconditional.

As his first assignment, Gord came out twice each week to package brochures for mailing. Over time, his leadership was evident in the way he set a steady pace for the group. After this job was completed, Gord painted fences and stained picnic tables. Because of his leadership abilities and meticulous work, he really did stand out. What was happening to Gord happens to anyone who experiences success. His self-esteem was rising and he was growing.

Over time, Gord's self-confidence began to bloom and he felt secure enough to let out a very well-kept secret that had not been revealed to many people. Gord can read, write and do math. This was wonderful news. At the same time, those of us who didn't know this all felt very humbled. Sometimes we think we are so aware and in touch with what is going on. The truth is, because something "seems" a certain way does not mean it "is" that way. Gord taught us a very important lesson.

With the support of those around him, Gord made a big step toward further independence. He bought a membership at the Y.M.C.A. and began working out on a regular basis. He also got a job on Saturdays. Gord is making some choices for himself that give his life shape and quality.

I chose to nominate Gord for the Provincial Outstanding Achievement Award in 1992 because he has covered a very long distance since he first came to volunteer. Quite regardless of the fact that he did not win the award, Gord's is a marvellous story of success. And the story continues.

*When I met Sandy, I found it hard to imagine that she
had been rejected. As the story was told, I found myself
getting more and more angry. Jennifer, the support
worker who wrote this story, raised her voice and
clenched her fists as she talked about it. She's still
astounded. Sandy sat calmly saying, "There's good and
bad in all people." This is not only Sandy's story, but
also Jennifer's and the other women who were part of
the struggle to be welcoming in this town.*

*I* met Sandy when she hired me as a support person. I remember being immediately
impressed by her ease at meeting people. We began talking about some new ways she
might begin to do this. Sandy expressed an interest in joining a women's group. We
looked around quite a bit before we found a club that seemed to be what Sandy was
looking for. I contacted the president. She was friendly and made it clear they were
eager for young members to energize their membership. She invited us to an
upcoming dinner meeting at a member's house to find out more. When we arrived, I
wasn't surprised to find Sandy already knew two of the ladies. As any true social
butterfly, Sandy flew into action!

Sandy continued to attend the next few meetings. I went with her the first few
times, mostly as a physical aide with stairs and the washroom. Soon, other members
of the club were offering Sandy any help she needed and I stopped going. One of the
club members was giving her a ride home after meetings. Eventually, Sandy decided
she would like to become a member of the club.

It was a real shock when I heard that there was some opposition to Sandy joining
the club. A member called me at home and had the gall to tell me that I would be
welcome as a member, but not Sandy. I remember her saying that if they let one
person who needs support in, they'll all come.

The club decided to have a vote at a special meeting to decide whether Sandy could
join. This was the final straw. No other member had been subjected to this humiliating

process. I was told the meeting was pretty tense, but in the end the group voted not to allow Sandy to join. I asked the president to explain their decision to Sandy. She didn't. Although I dreaded telling her, to me this was a clear human rights issue. Sandy had no wish to become a member in the midst of such turmoil and conflict.

The club lost out because Sandy had so much to offer. She had the time and was more than willing to help out at their thrift shop, which depends on volunteers. Prejudice is an ugly thing. It's frightening to me that people can be so fearful that a small thing like Sandra's membership application can explode into such a bizarre situation.

Even at this very low point, something special began to emerge. We learned that a few of the ladies in the group had been actively advocating for Sandy. In fact, one member who fought for Sandy to be allowed to join was told she herself wouldn't be allowed to vote. Members who had offered to help Sandy at the meetings were disappointed and angry at the club's decision. It became clear that those opposed to Sandy joining were a vocal minority who were powerful enough to sway the majority of members.

I remember feeling a great sense of renewed belief in the community when I was told the day after the special meeting that several members had decided to resign. They had told the group that they were disgusted with their attitude and would not be associated with an organization that treated people with so little respect. The club lost out because it was the younger members who had resigned. How ironic, in view of my first conversation with the club president; at that time she told me they were looking for young members to energize the membership.

Sandy does not have a prejudiced bone in her body. She has the wisdom to let go. She has forgiven. I'm not sure I have. Sandy has not let this rejection stop her. She is active in town and stays in touch with some of the women who resigned from the club. I realize that Sandy has probably gained more valuable ties than she lost by not being allowed to join the club.

*All of us face struggles to find our place in our communities. Steve saw there were barriers that stopped some of the town's residents from being included in local activities. He knew it wasn't up to somebody else to make things better. Steve felt he should be part of the action.*

*T*hinking back in my life, I realize there have been people who have worked hard to make our town a great place in which to live. They are the organizers and leaders of our community who have always worked to make sure there is a wide range of activities to choose. As a kid, I was never without things to do. Certainly, as an adult, there are lots of things people can do.

And yet, there is a group of people who are not included. Perhaps because of people's attitudes, perhaps they don't have the money, or perhaps they can't get into the building because they use a wheelchair. I'm not sure when I first became aware that there were many people in my community who didn't have the same opportunities that I did.

But it did become clear to me it was time to get involved in a way that I could try to make a difference. I became a board member for the local Association for Community Living and was asked to sit on a committee that promotes leisure activities. I remember going to my first committee meeting and noticing that each member represented a special group, organization, service club or sports club. In fact, the committee supported "special" group activities.

It has always bothered me that anyone who seems different, has to be labelled "special." In school, we have special education. In sports, we have special teams. Yet society endorses the idea that everyone is special. If we do believe that everyone is special, we need to refocus our attention to getting people involved. For our committee, it meant we had to drop all the labels.

With financial support from the Ministry of Tourism and Recreation, we were able to get started. Within a year, 72 people supported by the Association were actively participating in our town: church groups, baseball leagues, service clubs, art classes and much more. All this was done through staff supporting people to become connected on an individual basis.

At one point, the committee was approached to financially help one lady who had been travelling out of town to "special" riding stables. She needed funding to pay for staff to drive her 100 kilometres out of town to get there. We had a hard time with this one. First of all, why special? We decided to take a stand and help her find a local riding stable. This lady now rides at a farm five minutes, rather than one hour, outside of town. In fact, she works at the riding stable and enjoys riding on fair weather days. She loves horses! We are pleased for her, and us, that our beliefs had passed the test.

This success gave the committee momentum. We decided to tackle another big issue. The committee looked at accessibility. If people couldn't get into buildings, how could they participate? We initiated a task force that worked on making our Community Centre Complex accessible. This was a big job. However, within a year, actual renovations were taking place and people were able to get into the building.

Looking back, there were many times we as a committee didn't know exactly what we were doing. We survived our growing pains, but our greatest learning came from the challenges we faced!

Maybe it was the coming together of the right people, at the right time, who believed in making a difference. For whatever reason, I am honoured to be part of a group that believes in making our town a great place for everyone.

# coming home

To introduce the following stories about coming home from institutions, Elizabeth's sister says it best:

One of my favourite memories of my sister Elizabeth and I together happened at the beach. A friend of mine was there. She was wearing brown shoes. Elizabeth looked down and said, "Brown." While it might not sound like much, at 26-years-old, my sister had spoken spontaneously.

It comes back to me now, the simple word "brown" meant that there was more to my sister than I had seen. In all the visits, I only saw Elizabeth rocking in a chair, waiting for us to pick her up. Rocking and waiting is all I remember seeing her do. Her single word indicated hope. She could move forward. From then on, a place to sit and rock was not what I wanted for Elizabeth. But rather, a place to grow and learn.

*I listened to Elizabeth's sister, Cathy, as we looked through old family photographs. Seeing the smiling family grouped together gave me a warm feeling. Elizabeth's grandmother, aunt and uncle lived close by and helped support the parents. Nevertheless, Elizabeth left home at the age of six because it was much too difficult for the family to support her. This is Elizabeth's sister's story of the visits to her, over the years.*

*E*lizabeth looked so normal as a kid. I know there were problems when she was born. She had meningitis and was in the hospital. The doctors said she was profoundly retarded and she had seizures in her first year.

I remember riding in the car to visit her at the institution with my family. Elizabeth would always be sitting and rocking every time we went. I had the idea she had to live there because my parents could not control her at home. She would strike out at people and scream.

In the institution, Elizabeth seemed to have no life beyond the rocking and food. Maybe it was the medication she was on. When she moved to a different facility, it was quite a change. She was clean and neat, which is important to Elizabeth. Our mother is like that too. Very particular about her clothing and hair and how it all looks. That place taught her to recognize colours. She learned to say single words. She was always on a program, and she learned things.

She also adapted to her environment. For example, in a place with many people, you would tend to protect your food. You would have to eat fast before someone could take it from you. This is not what Elizabeth would do if she didn't have to. She liked to take her time with food if she could.

As an adult, Elizabeth moved to a group home. She loved having her hair done and being made up. I often saw the group home staff helping her with that. She started to talk in phrases and learned to ask questions.

She fights new things, but it is possible to decipher what she is afraid of by what she does. It is important to persevere with Elizabeth and spend time with her doing the things she likes. She makes her needs and wants known if you really listen. Elizabeth communicates with yelling and swearing when she is angry or afraid.

Going to get an annual physical proved too stressful, so Elizabeth went for her physical at a nearby institution. She did come back to the group home two months later, but she had regressed while she was away. Nine months later, when she had to have surgery, she again tried the town hospital. But, as before, it proved too stressful and she was transferred back to the institution's infirmary. This was the place where she lost ten years of learning. Elizabeth seems to be healing now, but there are a lot of scars.

From the institution, she moved to a different group home. I have learned you can tell a lot about a place by how it smells. Institutions smell of disinfectant and bleach. Home smells of cooking in the kitchen. The staff tell you all the places Elizabeth has gone and what she has done that week. I feel the government made a good decision to close institutions for people with developmental disabilities. People can't be expected to fit into spots. You have to adjust the situation for each person. I know Elizabeth has learned to relax her guard over the last few years in her new home. Let me tell an example.

A friend and I took Elizabeth out to McDonald's. I went to the washroom, and when I returned, I heard a little snicker. I lifted up my drink, and it was empty. She had played a joke on me. Wow! If I only knew then, what I know now. I would have asked much earlier for what Elizabeth needed to be better off. She would certainly have learned her colours before age 26!

*When I first met John, he had the distinction of having many outfits, but all were duplicates. Five pale green shirts, ten navy polyester pants, pairs of identical shoes and many same colour socks. This, of course, means easier sorting. Since that time, I have noticed a change in John. He is expressing his individuality in many different ways.*

*I* hope the bad times in my life are over. When I was born, they used forceps. When I was one-year-old, I had a very bad seizure. I was blue in the face for seven hours straight. A truck ran over me when I was seven, and broke my leg. Ever since, I have had this bad arm that doesn't move on its own. Some people say the accident led to more brain damage as well. I have had a bad time with my body. At least I could go to Friendship School which was good because I got to live at home with my family.

When I was 19, my body caught on fire. It was a bad fire. Seventy-five percent of my body was burnt badly and only 25 percent was left for me to live. If it hadn't been for my mom and dad, I would be dead. I was in and out of so many hospitals and had so much surgery, it was not funny at all. I feel bad that I was using the lighter and the fluid got all over me. My leg got infected and I had to have it amputated above my right knee. Now, I only have my right arm and my left leg that are whole.

I moved to the institution and I lived there for 16 years. It was strict and bossy. If I did not want to have a bath right then, they would give me the cold shower treatment and that was cruel to see. If I did anything wrong, they would put me in the time out room, locked up. Even the food was no good because it was all steamed. By the time it would get to our ward, it was cold and I did not want to eat it. My parents would bring me money and, in my spare time, I would go down to the cafeteria for hamburger and fries.

When the institution closed down, I moved into a group home, half an hour away from my family by car. Mom and Dad would come and see me and I would go home for holidays.

I was put back in the hospital for three months for assessments because the staff did not believe I had real seizures. I was not faking the seizures, but I decided not to get a shunt to drain the fluid, because it was not too bad. Then I would not have to have another operation.

Recently, I moved into an apartment with my roommate, Randy. I get along well with him and we can talk and joke about things. We go to People First meetings together every month. At the meetings, people talked a lot about moving into their own places. It helped me to hear everyone talk about the problems of looking for apartments, and how good it is to be able to move where you want to live. Since joining People First, I have been a Board member and also Vice-President in our local chapter.

People First is a self-advocacy group to help people get what they want. That could be a job that is real which you get real money for, not just six dollars a week like a workshop. The People First group helps us get our own apartments and it is also a way of meeting other people and making friends. We get to know each other better and we often sit down and make plans. Sometimes, we go out to supper, like Sean and I did this year, with Randy.

People First organizes conferences and I have travelled by Greyhound to many places. I went to Gananoque, Orangeville, Thunder Bay, Newmarket and Toronto. I love to travel and meet new people. Getting together with other people helps us to talk about our problems.

I like it now that I am in my own apartment and I have a part-time paid job. I still want a full-time office job and I am looking for one with my support worker.

My dad died a few years ago and I miss him. I don't go home on weekends except on holidays, but I am busy going out, attending meetings and getting things for my apartment. My life is different now that I can do what I want, and I can ask for more.

When I bought my first pair of blue jeans, I was so happy. But I can't wear them to work except on Fridays, because that's the rule at the office. That's the rule for all the employees, not just me. That's what I like about my life now.

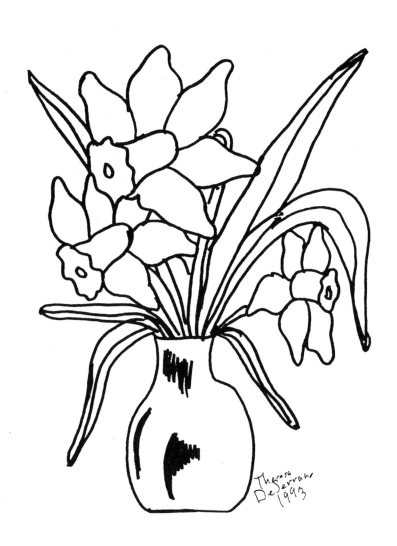

Theresa
DeSerrano
1993

*My greatest accomplishment so far in my life is losing 30 lbs. Losing this weight constantly reminds me who is in control of my life. I am!*

*I* was almost three years old when I was moved into an institution. I went to many hospitals but doctors did not express hope for me. I could kick them for that! I got bumped from city to city, facility to facility. I ended up living in an institution for 15 years, and then went to a nursing home for the following 16 years.

I remember the toughest times for me were when Mom and Dad took me back to the institution after each weekend at home. It was an empty feeling deep down in my stomach, the moment I heard those big doors lock behind them and they were gone. Holy cow! I was human like everyone else. I felt like I was fenced in and nobody cared.

Life in the institution was no picnic. When I got upset, I would go in the corner of the room and cry for hours. I was unable to tell people I did not want to be there. The staff never seemed to have enough time to sit and talk to me. There were so many others who needed their help.

I have many stories I could tell, but there is one I would like to share from my days in the institution.

It was early morning. I had finished my breakfast and was headed down to the sheltered workshop which was in the basement. I wheeled myself to the elevators. I was all alone. The elevator doors closed and it started to move.

Then all of a sudden, the elevator stopped. I was stuck. As I reached to take off my elevator key that hung around my neck, it fell out of my hands and down the crack of the elevator. I started to panic. There was a phone in the elevator but I could not reach it from my wheelchair. I started to sweat. My heart was pounding 90 miles an hour. I began yelling at the top of my lungs and, worst of all, I had to go to the bathroom! I could hear someone saying, "What's all the fuss?" Once I finally got out, I had to go back to my ward. I got heck for yelling and was given a cold shower because I had wet myself.

Maybe that's why I am always saying, "Sorry", to people who want to help me. I have finally stopped apologizing if I need help. Up until now, I was made to believe I was putting someone out if I needed assistance.

After living in the institution, I spent 16 years in a nursing home.

Finally, last year, I moved into my apartment with two other women. Life is different now. I am alive and happy.

I lost 30 pounds after I moved into my new home. I used to have to get up at the crack of dawn when I lived in the institutions, because that's when breakfast was served. By 10:00 a.m., I was hungry. Back in those days, I could not get through a day without at least one Mars Bar! Now I get up much later in the morning. I have a leisurely breakfast, enjoy a nice warm bath and then I am off to work.

I work at the town's Recreation Centre. I am the ticket taker for the noon hour swim. When I first started working at the Rec Centre, the building was not fully wheelchair accessible. Even though the support worker had cased it out before I started, people had overlooked the door openings into the bathrooms. They renovated. Now I can go to the bathroom without any problems. I am proud of that because I know that other people who use wheelchairs can use the Centre more often.

When I moved into my apartment, we had to look into getting a lift for my bathtub. Joy, a support worker, found out that these lifts were not that expensive and she took this information to the Rec Centre. She thought it would be a great idea to have a lift for the pool. She contacted the Lions Club and asked them if they would financially support putting this lift in the Rec Centre. They too thought it was great and gave money to the town so that a lift could be installed. Now, I not only work at the Rec Centre, but I get to swim there too! And so do others who need that lift.

At last year's staff Christmas party, it took four guys to carry me and my wheelchair up a flight of stairs. Although it was rather embarrassing, I have to admit I enjoyed those four good looking guys fussing over me. It was a great Christmas party!

The thing that I love best is not having to live with 60 other people anymore. I still have days that I get very weepy and I will barely say a word. At times like this, I know I can call on my staff. We can go into my room and talk. People are finally listening to me and I'm learning to express myself.

One time, I had a chance to help out at a Sunday School class. I told them about my life. I told them why my legs did not work. A little girl touched my knee and asked me, "Will I hurt you?" I told her, "No. I have wheels under my feet to get around." The little girl continued to sit close to me. I can honestly say I was able to remove some of that little girl's fear that morning.

People still say, "Oh, I feel so sorry for you." But I tell them they don't need to. I am not mad at people who don't understand. I need friends, not pity. I tell them that I volunteer at a nursing home once a week. I visit with people who do not have much to look forward to. I can relate to what those people in the nursing home are experiencing.

For me, life is so much better now. I can choose how I want to spend my life. I am able to pick out what I want to wear, mostly purple clothes because that's my favourite colour. I have a part-time job. I am a board member of the agency I belong to. I have become close to my brother Bill, who I can call anytime and he visits me often.

Now, I'm more aware of my responsibilities and what I can do with the help of staff who live in my new home. Starting something new is a scary thing. Changes are scary too. I'm willing to try new things now, because I know it gets smoother as I go along. I like my life, now that it's easier for me to voice my opinion. I was scared to do that before.

People tell me I have a heart of gold. That is probably why I feel badly when my mom does not agree with the decisions I make sometimes. There have been times when she has not liked the clothes I wear. Mom and I have grown to understand each other this past year. I like speaking up for myself. My dream is to purchase an electric wheelchair so I do not have to rely on others to take me everywhere. I can see, eventually, going downtown shopping all by myself.

It goes back to losing weight. I like having the power to make my own decisions and having control over my own life. I can be in a room full of chocolate bars and I can walk away from them. Can you?

# *p.s.*

As Peter Park said at the beginning of this book, listening is the key. Hearing goes in one ear and out the other. Listening is stopping in the middle and taking action.

On our journey with ***Her shoes are brown and other stories***, we have seen triumphs and many successes. People are taking action by turning their beliefs into reality by trusting themselves and others.

In our travels, we spoke to many people. They told different stories of the trials toward triumph. We recognize there is often a gap between philosophy and action. This gap separates the belief that all people can contribute to their communities, and the act of supporting each other to make it happen. We also heard about the struggles to jump that gap. Those thoughts, brainstorms, notes, concerns, impressions, beliefs and viewpoints are compiled in ***Jumping the gap - more stories and ideas.*** Read it and leap!

Comments, ideas, more stories? Please write or tape your thoughts and send them to us:

STORIES
Community Involvement Council
Box 344
Tillsonburg, Ontario
N4G 4H8